CALL OF THE WILD

Steve Barlow and Steve Skidmore

Illustrated by Alex Lopez

Franklin Watts
First published in Great Britain in 2015 by The Watts Publishing Group

Credits
Series Editor: Adrian Cole
Design Manager: Peter Scoulding
Cover Designer: Cathryn Gilbert
Illustrations: Alex Lopez

HB ISBN 978 1 4451 4390 3
PB ISBN 978 1 4451 4392 7
Library ebook ISBN 978 1 4451 4391 0

Printed in China.

Franklin Watts
An imprint of
Hachette Children's Group
Part of The Watts Publishing Group
Carmelite House
50 Victoria Embankment
London EC4Y 0DZ

An Hachette UK Company
www.hachette.co.uk

www.franklinwatts.co.uk

Lin is a werewolf.

Danny is a demon.

Sam is a zombie.

The three friends go to Hangem High School.

They don't want people to know they are monsters.

9

"Come with me," said Mr Broad. "The rangers will talk about the project."

The class followed Mr Broad. But Lin didn't move. She gave a groan. "Wolves? Oh, no!"

Sam stopped and stared at her. "What's wrong?"

"She's a werewolf!" said Danny. "Being around wolves makes her want to change. Lin, you must not change into a werewolf..."

11

Sam groaned. "Mr Broad will find out Lin is a werewolf!"

"No he won't! We'll get her back before he finds out!" Danny jumped at the fence. "We're going after her! Help me up."

Sam and Danny crept towards the wolf.

"Call her," said Danny. "Click your fingers — like this."

"I can't," moaned Sam, "they will fall off!"

Just then...

21

Lin grabbed Sam's leg and followed Sam and Danny over the fence. She changed back to human form.

28

29